# MILLIE AND MO DREAM BIG

*Reagan,*
*Always chase your Dreams!*
*DREAM BIG!*
*Morris King*

by Morris King

Illustrated by Ricky and Mary Nobile

PAGE PUBLISHING, INC.
Conneaut Lake, PA

First originally published by Page Publishing 2019

ISBN 978-1-68456-504-7 (pbk)
ISBN 978-1-64584-471-6 (hc)
ISBN 978-1-68456-505-4 (digital)

Printed in the United States of America

This book
belongs to

_____

It has been said that the two most important days in our lives are the day we are born and the day we find out why.

Although we are all born with the ability to dream, living the life of our dreams requires us to take action. My mom and dad always empowered our family to chase our dreams, offering encouragement, setting examples, and teaching faith that all things are possible. They challenged us to explore opportunities and try new things while instilling a solid work ethic that would carry us through life. Understanding that sometimes falling down is part of life and getting back up is living, they seemed to always know when to stand behind us and when to stand in front. This book is dedicated to my mom and dad. Thanks for all you've done and for always telling us to dream big, stand tall, and keep moving forward!

Morris King

Hello! My name is Millie. I love dreaming of fun things to do and sharing them with my friends.

I'd like you to meet my best friend, Mo!
We enjoy exploring and looking for new
adventures!

Every morning, we go for a walk and say hello to all the animals that live around our house.

Sometimes, we go for a ride in the canoe. It's fun to look for wildlife as the water splashes on my face.

We always stop and play in the water. The animals that live by the lake love to watch me chase the ball!

Swimming is so much fun! Do you like to swim?

Watching fish jump out of the water is also exciting! Have you ever been fishing?

After a long day of activities, one of my favorite things to do is take a nap and dream of new adventures.

I dream of jumping out of an airplane and parachuting to the ground!

What a great adventure it would be to help
keep our country safe!

One day, I would like to visit a hospital. I can help someone feel better and bring a smile to their face.

Helping others is a wonderful thing to do!
Do you like to help people?

I dream of using my nose to find a lost person and reunite them with their family!

Maybe I could use my eyes to help someone safely cross the street!

I can run faster and jump higher than any dog in the world!

With all my abilities, I dream of one day entering the Olympics and winning a gold medal!

In the spring, it would be fun to plant a garden and watch it grow.

Maybe we can work on a farm and help a cowboy round up his cattle!

In the fall, we can harvest pumpkins and go on a hayride! Have you ever been on a hayride?

When it's cold, I will watch ducks and geese fly high in the sky!

There are so many places to visit and things I would like to do! How about you?

Chasing dreams is always a race full of adventure!

If you work hard and have courage to chase your dreams, one day, all your dreams may come true. What dreams would you like to come true for you?

Morris and Millie

# About the Author

Morris King grew up in Huntsville, Alabama. When Morris was twelve years old, his parents purchased a Labrador retriever puppy, which ignited his passion for training dogs. Morris always enjoyed the stories people shared about their pets and stood intrigued at the tasks a dog could perform. He has seen how our lives are enhanced through the intelligence of these magnificent creatures, whether they are working in service or hanging out with the family. These animals can unlock the boundaries we often set for ourselves and help us overcome life's obstacles. Morris wrote this book to encourage children to chase their dreams and to honor the animals that prove to us that anything is possible. DREAM BIG!

Cousins Morris King and Ricky and Mary Nobile collaborated to bring this story of *Millie and Mo* to life.

## The Illustrators

Ricky Nobile and his wife, Mary, teamed up to create the artwork in this book and help Morris tell his story of Millie and Mo. Ricky is a cartoonist, and Mary is a graphic artist. Ricky's editorial cartoons are featured in forty Mississippi newspapers weekly, have been featured in the *Harvard Political Review*, and Best Editorial Cartoons of the Year. Ricky is also a member of the Association of American Editorial Cartoonists. Ricky and Mary are pleased to be part of this special book and its message: DREAM BIG!

CPSIA information can be obtained
at www.ICGtesting.com
Printed in the USA
LVHW062155181219
641033LV00005B/129/P